MYSTERY
AT THE
WASHINGTON
MONUMENT

by **Ron Roy**
illustrated by **Timothy Bush**

A STEPPING STONE BOOK™

Random House New York

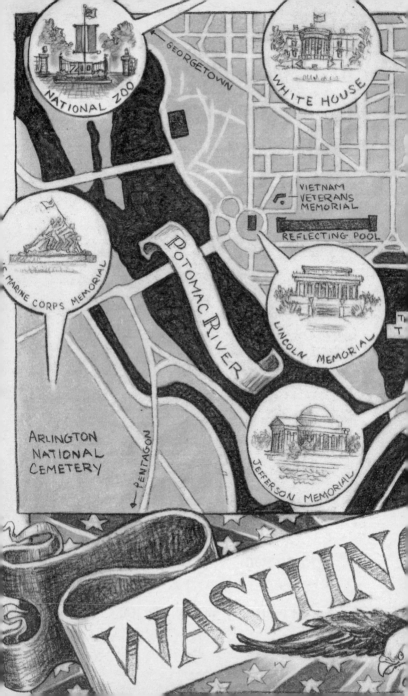

This is dedicated to Lloyd Emerick and his grandsons, Erik and Seth Gebel.
—R.R.

Photo credits: p. 88 bottom, courtesy of the National Park Service; p. 88 top and p. 89, courtesy of the Library of Congress.

Text copyright © 2007 by Ron Roy
Illustrations copyright © 2007 by Timothy Bush
Cover illustration copyright © 2009 by Greg Swearingen

Visit us on the Web!
www.steppingstonesbooks.com
www.randomhouse.com/kids

Educators and librarians, for a variety of teaching tools, visit us at www.randomhouse.com/teachers

Library of Congress Cataloging-in-Publication Data
Roy, Ron.
Mystery at the Washington Monument / by Ron Roy ; illustrated by Timothy Bush.
   p.   cm. — (Capital mysteries ; 8)
"Stepping Stone book."
Summary: When KC and Marshall see lights flickering at night in the Washington Monument, their investigation turns up a monkey, a hole in one of the monument stones, and a hundred-year-old mystery.
ISBN 978-0-375-83970-2 (pbk.) — ISBN 978-0-375-93970-9 (lib. bdg.)
[1. Monkeys—Fiction. 2. Stealing—Fiction. 3. Washington (D.C.)—Fiction. 4. Mystery and detective stories.] I. Bush, Timothy, ill. II. Title.
PZ7.R8139Mys 2007 [Fic]—dc22 2006029616

Printed in the United States of America
15 14 13 12 11 10 9

Contents

1
Strange Lights

KC snuggled deeper inside her sleeping bag. She was camping out on the White House lawn with her best friend, Marshall Li. KC could smell the grass and the rosebushes. The traffic on Pennsylvania Avenue made a humming sound from the other side of the tall hedges. Fireflies danced in the bushes.

"Why does the Washington Monument have those flashing red and white lights?" Marshall asked. He was sitting up in his sleeping bag a few feet away.

"It only has red lights," KC said. "I think that's so airplanes won't hit it." She rolled over to look at the tall Monument. It was white against the night sky. At the top, red lights blinked on and off.

"KC, they're red and white," Marshall said, pointing. "Look."

"They're red, Marsh—" KC stopped speaking. Marshall was right. The red lights were flashing, but KC could also see white light in the windows at the top of the Monument. The white light seemed to move around. Sometimes it was bright. Sometimes it was just a glow.

"It looks like someone with a flashlight," Marshall said.

KC shook her head. "The Monument is closed at night," she said, climbing out of her sleeping bag. She walked toward the hedges.

"Well, someone is up there," Marshall insisted.

KC watched the white light. It seemed to move from window to window. "Let's go find out what it is!" KC said. She grabbed her flashlight.

"Now?" Marshall asked. He was standing up, pulling on his sneakers.

KC wanted to be a TV reporter when she grew up. She was curious about everything. She was especially curious about things that were strange, like those dancing white lights. But she knew her mom would kill her if she went walking around the city at night. With a sigh, she turned off the flashlight.

"We can go on one of the tours tomorrow and look around inside the Monument," KC said.

"Look around for what?" Marshall asked.

"A ghoooosssst," KC whispered as she crawled back into her sleeping bag.

After breakfast the next morning, KC and Marshall walked to the Washington Monument. A sign on a booth said that tickets for the tours were free. KC asked for two tickets for the nine o'clock tour. A park ranger in a gray uniform handed her the tickets and a pamphlet. His name tag said BUTCH.

Marshall stared up at the Monument. "Wow, how tall do you think it is?" he asked.

KC checked the pamphlet. It had a list of facts about the Washington Monument. "Five hundred and fifty-five feet," she answered, "and five inches."

"How do they know that?" Marshall asked. "I mean, how could they measure it? They'd need a really big ruler!"

KC shrugged. "No idea. Let's ask when we get inside," she said.

At nine, another park ranger opened the door at the base of the Monument. "Hi, my name is Opal," she said. "I'm your tour guide today." She took tickets and led the small group to the elevator.

"I thought we had to climb the stairs," Marshall said to the park ranger as they waited for the elevator.

Opal smiled. "Not anymore," she said. "There are almost nine hundred steps. Until around 1970, you had a choice. You could either climb the stairs or take the elevator. But a few people were breaking off pieces of the memorial stones to take as souvenirs. Now you can only go up in the elevator."

"What are the memorial stones?" a man asked.

"When the Monument was being built, many countries sent us huge stones to put inside," the ranger explained. "Our own states also sent stones. In all, there are one hundred ninety-two memorial stones. You'll get to see them when we come down in the elevator."

The elevator door opened and everyone stepped inside.

"The ride up is fast," Opal said. "But on the way down, it will be slower so you can see the stones."

The door closed and KC felt a jolt as the elevator rose quickly. A minute later, the door opened again. "This is the observation deck," Opal said. "You just climbed five hundred feet in seventy seconds! Enjoy the view. The next trip down is in ten minutes."

The tourists walked to the windows that looked out on Washington, D.C. The windows were on each side—north, south, east, and west. Each window offered a spectacular view of the buildings, streets, and parks. Tiny cars and buses darted about like bugs. People walking on the ground looked like ants.

KC stood next to the north window. "Look, Marsh!" She pointed at the lawn in front of the White House. "That's where we were last night. Those weird lights must have shone through this window!"

"Cool!" Marshall said. "If anyone was

up here last night, I wonder if they saw us on the lawn."

KC looked at Marshall. "I never thought about that," she said. She glanced around the observation deck.

Had someone been creeping around in here with a flashlight last night? Did they also have a telescope or binoculars? Were they watching the White House?

"Marsh!" KC hissed. "Maybe someone climbed up here to spy on the president!"

2
Weird Noises

"Don't be silly. How could anyone spy on the president from up here?" Marshall asked. "KC, you're always jumping to conclusions. There could be lots of explanations for the lights we saw last night."

"Oh yeah?" KC said. "Like what?"

"Maybe something in the Monument was broken, and they were fixing it," Marshall offered.

"Late at night?" KC said. "Why not wait till daytime?"

Marshall went on. "Maybe it was a party," he said. "Or a private tour for some important person."

They walked from window to window. KC half listened to him. She kept her eyes open for anything unusual. Over her head, the ceiling rose to a point. It was dark at the top. The walls were smooth marble. And she saw no lights at all, not flickering ones, not regular ones.

"Do you know how they measured the Monument to find out how tall it is?" Marshall asked Opal.

"Hmmm, I'm not sure," Opal said. "Ask Jennifer. She might know." She pointed across the observation deck.

A female park ranger was selling maps and books about the Monument at a small counter near the elevator door. An open bag of peanuts sat on the counter. Next to the bag was a small pile of empty shells.

Marshall repeated his question.

The woman named Jennifer swallowed the peanut she'd been chewing. "Gee, I don't know," she said. "That's a good question. No one ever asked me that before."

Suddenly the elevator door opened. "Going down!" a different ranger said. It was Butch, who'd given them tickets earlier.

KC and Marshall joined a few other people who had decided to leave the observation deck.

"Be sure to notice the memorial stones," Butch said.

The elevator began to descend slowly. Through the glass walls, KC could see the stones. Most had words or images carved into them. KC tried to make out some of the words, but she got dizzy trying to read while the elevator was moving.

"These stones came from all the states and many foreign countries," Butch said. "Even the Pope sent one from Rome."

"Are the stones valuable?" a woman in the elevator asked.

"Some are," Butch said. "The one from Alaska is solid jade!"

When the elevator reached the bottom, everyone got out. KC hung back. "Excuse me," she said to Butch. "My friend and I were camping on my lawn last night, and we saw a white light coming from the top windows. Do you know what that was?"

Butch looked down at KC and Marshall. "Do you remember what time it was?" he asked.

"Around ten o'clock," KC said. "It wasn't a strong light, just sort of glowy."

"Like someone with a flashlight," Marshall added.

Butch frowned. He seemed to think something over. "Tell you what, meet me at one of the picnic tables in ten minutes," he said. "I'll be taking my break, and we can talk some more."

Butch walked into an office that said EMPLOYEES ONLY on the door. KC raised her eyebrows at Marshall. "That sounded strange," she said. "He must know something about those white lights!" They went outside, found an empty picnic table, and sat to wait for the ranger.

The Monument's shadow fell on the lawn in front of them. "Maybe they measured the shadow to tell how tall the Monument is," Marshall suggested.

"But, Marsh, the shadow would be

shorter or longer when the sun was higher or lower in the sky," KC said. She grinned. "You know, when the earth moves."

"Yeah, I get it," Marsh said.

Just then Butch joined them. He sat and opened a brown paper bag. "Pardon me if I eat in front of you," he said. "I only get fifteen minutes and I forgot to eat breakfast."

"We don't mind," KC said.

Butch pulled a cheese sandwich and a bottle of juice from the bag. He took a big bite of the sandwich. "So you saw lights in the windows last night?" he asked as he chewed.

KC nodded. "We were having a sleep-out on the White House lawn," she told him.

Butch stopped eating. The look on his

face changed. "You slept on the White House lawn?" he asked.

Marshall laughed. "She's telling the truth," he said. "The president is her stepfather."

"Oh yeah, I read the president's new wife had a daughter," Butch said, tipping his sandwich toward KC. "And you're her!"

"I'm her," KC said. "My name is Katherine Christine Corcoran, but everyone calls me KC."

"And I'm Marshall Li," Marshall said.

Butch nodded. "I'm Lloyd Emerick, but you can call me Butch." He set his sandwich on the bag and wiped his mouth on a paper napkin. "I think someone was inside the Monument last night. This morning, I found some small pieces of plaster on the floor," he said.

"Maybe someone was trying to steal a memorial stone!" KC said.

Butch shook his head. "That would be impossible," he said. "The stones are really big and heavy. They're also concreted into the walls."

Butch sipped some juice. "There's something else weird," he said after a minute. "I heard an awful screeching sound this morning. It was like a big bird." Butch laughed. "I was pretty spooked," he said. "I don't believe in ghosts, but you never know."

KC remembered the glowing lights. She didn't believe in ghosts either, and she'd never heard of a bird that glowed in the dark!

"Could we see that stuff you found?" she asked.

"Yeah, I guess it would be okay," Butch said. "Come on."

The ranger bagged his snack and led the kids to a small room inside the Monument. He unlocked the door. There was a workbench in the middle of the room, and shelves lined all the walls. The shelves held cans of paint, cleaning supplies, and tools.

On the bench was a small pile of broken plaster. KC picked up one of the pieces. It was white on one side and gray on the other. "Where did you find it?" she asked.

Butch pointed toward the ceiling. "Up there, a few hundred steps," he said. "Feel like doing some climbing?"

"Sure!" Marshall said.

KC put the plaster piece in her pocket.

Butch unlocked the gate to the stairs. The Monument's inside walls were on their left as they climbed. A metal railing was opposite the walls.

Marshall stopped and stared up into the darkness. "How many stairs are there altogether?" he asked.

"Eight hundred and ninety-seven," Butch said. "In the old days, before the elevator was put in, a lot of tourists tried to walk up. Some of them gave up and turned around."

The kids climbed the first of many flights. They were able to look at some of the memorial stones up close. KC paused in front of a four-foot-long stone with the word *Maine* carved into its surface. Smaller carvings of animals and trees surrounded the state's name.

"That one is granite," Butch said. "See what I mean about how big these are? Of course, some are smaller. But they're all at least a foot thick. Trust me, without dynamite, no one is getting one of these babies out of here!"

They moved on. After climbing for five more minutes, they stopped. "I found the pieces right here," Butch said. He pointed to the floor.

Over the spot was a stone that said STATE OF WASHINGTON. Each letter was as big as KC's hand.

"What's this?" Marshall said, bending down. He picked up a peanut shell.

"I didn't see that before," Butch said.

Marshall checked for a trash can but didn't see one. He dropped the peanut shell into his pocket.

KC looked up at the stone from Washington State. "It's huge!" she said.

"Yep, this one is about four feet wide and two feet high," Butch said.

KC stood on her tiptoes to get a better view. "I think something is wrong with one of the letters," she said. "See the *o* in *Washington*? It's black, and the rest of the letters are gray."

Butch peered up at the letter. "I'll be darned," he said. "It looks like there's a hole where the *o* should be!"

"Maybe that's what the plaster came from," KC said.

"I'll have to get my boss," Butch said.

He left the kids and hoofed it down the way they'd just come.

KC was staring up at the Washington State memorial stone when Butch came back. He was out of breath and carrying a small ladder. Behind him was another park ranger. He had short gray hair and a pointy nose.

Butch leaned the ladder against the wall. "Kids, this is my boss, Dr. Grift," Butch said. "Boss, this is KC and Marshall. KC is the president's stepdaughter!"

"How do you do?" Dr. Grift said. "Now what's this about the Washington stone?"

KC pointed up at the letter *o*.

Dr. Grift looked up. "How odd," he said. "Butch, please climb up there and examine the stone."

Butch climbed to the top rung of the ladder. "Boss, there's a round hole cut right into the stone!" he said.

3
Monkey in the Monument

"A hole?" Dr. Grift said. "What kind of hole? Is there anything in it?"

Butch poked a finger into the hole. "Nothing but a few pieces of plaster," he said. He climbed down the ladder and showed them what he had found.

"That's the same kind of plaster you found on the floor, right?" Marshall said.

KC dug the other plaster bit from her pocket. "They *are* the same," she said.

"This is very distressing," Dr. Grift said. "Damaged memorial stones in the Washington Monument!"

Just as Dr. Grift spoke, something fell

on Marshall's head. He reached up and pulled a peanut shell from his hair.

"Where did that come from?" KC asked him.

"Another peanut shell!" Butch said.

"Now what?" Dr. Grift sighed.

They all looked up.

"Oh my gosh!" KC cried. Twenty feet above their heads, a small brown monkey sat perched on the railing. It had a long tail, tiny hands, and a round, curious face. The monkey stared down at them, blinking its shiny black eyes.

"Is that what I think it is?" Butch asked.

"It's a monkey!" yelled Marshall.

"I don't believe this," moaned Dr. Grift. "What's a monkey doing in the Washington Monument?"

"Beats me, Boss," Butch said.

They were all quiet for a moment.

"Should we try to catch him?" KC asked.

"I wish I had a banana," Marshall said.

The monkey began making chirping noises. Suddenly it leaped twenty feet down and landed on Butch's chest. Butch looked totally surprised. He petted the monkey gently while it snuggled into his shirt.

"We can't have a monkey living in the Monument!" Dr. Grift said. His face had turned red.

"I know, Boss," Butch said. "I wonder how it got in here!"

"Perhaps some tourist snuck it in," Dr. Grift said. "But that doesn't matter. It has to leave now! Those things have fleas!"

"Most monkeys are very clean," said Marshall. He petted the monkey's tail.

"Still, the animal has to go," Dr. Grift insisted.

"I can bring it with me to the White House," KC said. "The president really likes animals."

Butch and Dr. Grift looked at KC.

"We already have a dog and three cats," KC told them.

Dr. Grift rubbed his hands over his face. "Thank you, Miss Thornton," he said. "If you can take the monkey to the White House, that would be a help."

"My last name is actually Corcoran," KC said. She took the monkey from Butch and nestled it in her arms. The monkey didn't seem afraid. "And I'll tell the president about the hole in the stone."

"Um, yes, of course he'll have to know," Dr. Grift mumbled.

Butch carried the ladder down the stairs, with Dr. Grift at his heels. KC and Marshall followed them.

"Want to carry him?" KC asked.

"Sure!" Marshall said, reaching his arms out. "Come to Uncle Marshall." The monkey climbed onto him. It stuck a tiny paw into Marshall's pocket and pulled out the peanut shell.

He chewed on the empty shell for a few seconds, then spit it out.

When the kids reached the bottom of the stairs, Butch and Dr. Grift were nowhere in sight. The ranger named Opal was leading a group of tourists toward the elevator.

Suddenly the monkey shrieked and

began struggling to get out of Marshall's arms.

The tourists looked up. "Look, a monkey!" one of them cried.

"Why is there a monkey in the Washington Monument?" another tourist asked.

"Please step into the elevator," Opal said.

They stepped in, the door closed, and KC heard the whirring sound as the elevator rose.

Marshall stroked the monkey's back. "He's trembling," Marshall said. "I guess he doesn't like tourists."

"Come on," KC said. "Let's take him home. And we have to name him. We can't just call him Monkey!"

"Any ideas?" Marshall asked.

"Yeah. Let's call him Marshall," KC teased.

"Very funny," Marshall said. "But I think we should name him Washington."

KC smiled. "Excellent!" she said.

4

Too Many Mysteries

KC and Marshall walked back to the White House.

"Come on, Marsh, let's go online and find out what kind of monkey Washington is," KC said when they were inside.

"He's a spider monkey," Marshall said.

KC laughed. "Of course you'd think that," she said. Marshall loved anything with more than four legs—bugs, spiders, you name it.

"No, really! They're called spider monkeys because they have long, skinny legs like spiders," he told KC. "They eat fruit and insects."

The kids went to KC's room. Marshall put the monkey on the bed. Right away Washington hopped off and began exploring. He picked up things, tasted them, shook them, smacked them together.

KC sat down and turned on the computer. Over her desk was a framed map of Washington, D.C. Marshall pulled up a second chair. "Should I search for all monkeys?" she asked Marshall.

"Naw, there are too many different kinds," he said. "Why not type in *spider monkey* and see what you get?"

In a few seconds, they were looking at a Web site about spider monkeys. There was a picture of a monkey that looked exactly like Washington.

"You were right, Marsh," KC said.

"Told you so," Marshall said with a grin.

Both kids read the page silently. "It says spider monkeys can even grab things with their tails!" KC said.

Marshall pointed to the screen. "Look, if you click on that button, we can hear what spider monkeys sound like," he said.

"Cool!" KC clicked the mouse, and the room filled with chirping and squeaking noises. Washington leaped through the air and landed on the desk. He put his tiny hands on the computer and listened. His eyes were wide. He began to make his own squeaky noises.

KC clicked again, and the monkey sounds went away. "I don't want him to get sad," she told Marshall. "He probably thought he was back home again."

Washington stood on his back legs and rested his front paws on the framed map.

He put his nose against the glass where the word *WASHINGTON* was printed in block letters.

"Look! He can read his name!" KC joked.

"Ha-ha," Marshall said. "Why—"

SMASH!

Marshall and KC whipped around.

Washington was holding a paperweight in both hands. He had smacked it against the map. The glass had cracked.

"Washington, no!" KC said. She took the paperweight away from him. "Bad monkey!"

"Gee, maybe he doesn't like his name after all," Marshall said.

Washington tapped on the glass with his paws, over and over.

Marshall picked up Washington and

carried him to the bed. The monkey jumped right off and leaped back onto KC's desk. He again began tapping on the map of Washington, D.C.

"Maybe he really *can* read his name," KC said. She wasn't joking anymore.

She and Marshall stared at each other for a minute. Could this monkey read?

"I know how we can test him," Marshall said slowly. "Come on!"

Marshall carried Washington to a hallway where there was no furniture. A red carpet ran the length of the hall. The only objects were pictures on the walls and a long row of statues of past presidents. Each marble statue sat on a pedestal. The president's name was carved into the base of the statue.

"Okay, I'm going to put him down and

see what he does," Marshall said. He set Washington on the floor.

Washington scampered around for a few minutes. Every time he came close to the statue of George Washington, KC and Marshall held their breath. But every time, the monkey ran right past the statue.

"Oh well," Marshall said, "I guess we were wrong."

"Wait!" KC shouted. "Look!"

Washington had leaped onto the statue of George Washington. The base had WASHINGTON written in large letters. The monkey started tapping it.

Marshall scooped Washington off the pedestal and set him on his shoulder.

"Marsh, put him down again," KC said.

Marshall bent to set Washington on the floor.

"No, not there, take him way down at the end, next to the statue of Thomas Jefferson," KC said.

Marshall carried Washington about thirty feet down the hall. When he set him on the carpet, Washington ran back to the George Washington statue. Again he climbed up on the pedestal. Again he started slapping his paws against the president's name.

Marshall plucked Washington from the pedestal. "Maybe he's trying to tell us that he doesn't like George Washington," he said. "Or Washington, D.C.," he added, remembering the map.

"No, Marshall, I think he likes Washington just fine," KC said. "And I think I've just figured out one of our mysteries!"

5
Monkey See, Monkey Do

Marshall sat on the floor with the monkey in his lap. "I don't get it," he said.

KC dropped down next to Marshall. "In my room a few minutes ago, he hit the map on the word *Washington,* right?" she asked.

Marshall nodded.

"And just now, he tapped the name Washington on the statue," KC went on. "With all these other presidents standing around, he picked Washington."

Marshall just looked at KC. "So what does that have to do with our mystery?" he asked.

"Marsh, back in the Monument, which memorial stone had a hole in it?" KC asked.

"The one from Washington State," he said. "Oh my gosh!"

"Here's what I think," KC said, petting Washington. "I think someone snuck this monkey into the Monument last night. The light we saw must have been from a flashlight."

"Okay, I'm with you," Marshall said.

"That person had trained Washington to climb up to that state of Washington memorial stone and hit on the *o*," KC continued. "When he smacked the *o*, he broke through it. That's what made the broken plaster that Butch showed us."

"Holy moly!" Marshall said. "But why would someone do that?"

"There must have been something hidden in that hole!" KC said. "Something important enough to sneak in with a trained monkey to get it."

"Like what? Gold? Money? Jewels?" Marshall's eyes lit up.

KC shrugged. She had no idea what was hidden in the hole.

"I wonder who trained him to do that," KC went on.

"I'll bet it's hard to train a monkey," Marshall said. He stroked Washington's thin arms. The monkey pulled his right arm away.

"Hey, what's wrong?" Marshall asked the monkey. "Does something hurt?"

When KC and Marshall tried to examine the arm, Washington pulled away again. He began to tremble.

"Maybe he hurt it banging against the statue," KC suggested.

"Should we take him to a vet?" Marshall asked.

"I guess so," KC said. "But where can we find a vet who treats monkeys?"

"Easy," Marshall said. He slung one arm around KC's shoulders. "At the National Zoo, right here in D.C."

KC grinned at Marshall. "Sometimes you're brilliant!" she said.

"You mean sometimes I'm *not* brilliant?" Marshall teased.

KC and Marshall took Washington back to KC's room. KC called the National Zoo and asked for a monkey vet.

She told someone she had a spider monkey with a hurt arm.

"My name is KC Corcoran," she added.

"My stepfather is President Thornton."

A minute later, she hung up. She had a big smile on her face. "Dr. Tutu is going to meet us at the main gate," she said.

"How will we get Washington there?" Marshall asked. "I don't know if they allow monkeys on the Metro trains."

"I know," KC said. She grabbed her backpack and unzipped the top compartment. She lined it with an old sweatshirt and set Washington down inside.

The monkey curled into a ball and closed its eyes.

"He likes it in there!" KC said.

"Maybe it reminds him of the nest where he was born," Marshall suggested.

The kids took the Metro train. They got off at the zoo stop. It was a ten-minute walk to the zoo.

Even outside the gate, the sweet smell of wild animals and exotic plants told them they were getting close.

A tall man wearing shorts and a tropical shirt waited under a tree. Around his neck was a thick necklace of colored beads. The necklace shone against his dark skin.

KC and Marshall approached the man. "Hi, I'm KC, and this is Marshall," KC said.

"And I am Dr. Tutu," the man said. "Where is your little friend?"

KC opened her backpack. Washington was sound asleep on her sweatshirt.

"Delightful," Dr. Tutu said. "Follow me to my office, please."

They passed the elephant enclosure. Marshall laughed when he saw a long trunk appear over the wall.

Dr. Tutu's office was in a small white building near the monkey house. Flowers lined a short path to the front steps. Two rocking chairs sat on the porch, nestled among potted plants.

Dr. Tutu held the door open, and the kids trooped inside. "Please put your backpack on the examining table," Dr. Tutu said.

He opened the pack and gently set Washington on the table. The monkey blinked his eyes and yawned.

"These are charming little monkeys, but they are thieves," Dr. Tutu said. "They steal birds' eggs right out of the nests. They also take shiny objects, so tell the president to hide his jewelry!"

Dr. Tutu looked in Washington's eyes and mouth. He examined his ears, fingers, toes, and even his long tail. He took his temperature and listened to his heart with a stethoscope.

"This fellow seems very healthy," Dr. Tutu said. "Which arm did you say was bothering him?"

"The right one," Marshall said.

Dr. Tutu touched the arm, and Washington pulled it away.

"I'll need some X-rays," Dr. Tutu said.

He set Washington on an X-ray table and took the pictures. Soon he was studying the X-rays. He pointed to a thin line crossing one of the bones.

"This is the ulna bone, and it has a fracture," Dr. Tutu said. "The bone was set, but it hasn't quite healed. Some vet has done a fine job with it. Has he been banging against anything with this arm?"

The kids quickly told him the story of how they found Washington inside the Washington Monument. They filled him in on how the monkey liked to bang against pictures and statues.

"Fascinating," Dr. Tutu said. "I hope you solve your mystery, but keep this little fellow quiet until his arm is completely healed."

KC had an idea. "Can we find out who the other vet is, the one who set Washington's arm?" she asked.

Dr. Tutu looked at her. "Is this important?" he asked.

KC told him they were trying to figure out who trained Washington to find the hidden hole in the memorial stone.

"I love mysteries!" Dr. Tutu said, walking over to his desk. He turned on his computer as KC and Marshall watched.

"It would most likely be a local vet," he mumbled as he typed in a few commands. "We all keep records on the exotic animals that we treat, like monkeys, parrots, and snakes."

After a few minutes, he sat back. "Yes, the vet is Dr. Leslie Warren. I know her well."

"She fixed Washington's arm?" asked Marshall.

Dr. Tutu nodded his head. "About ten weeks ago. Shall I call her?"

"That would be excellent!" KC said.

Dr. Tutu reached for his telephone and dialed a number. "Hello, Leslie? Phillip Tutu here. Do you remember setting the right ulna in a spider monkey a few months back? You do? Any chance you have the owner's name?" Dr. Tutu winked at KC and Marshall. "Thank you, Leslie," he said, then hung up.

"Your monkey was owned by a D. Dimm," Dr. Tutu said. "At least Dimm is the name Dr. Warren has in her book. She didn't meet the owner herself."

The kids thanked Dr. Tutu. KC put Washington into her backpack, and they headed back toward the zoo exit.

"Well, now what?" Marshall asked. "We still don't know who this Dimm person is, except that he or she probably trained Washington and brought him into the Monument."

"We don't know a lot of things," KC said. "Like how someone could drill a hole in that stone. Or what they hid in it. Or when, for that matter."

"I wonder when the stone was put into the Washington Monument," Marshall said.

"They were put in after the Monument was built," KC said. She remembered what she'd read in the pamphlet.

"Why would someone drill a hole in the stone, cover it over with plaster, then train a monkey to break it open again?" Marshall asked. "It doesn't make any sense."

"It makes sense if the person who drilled the hole isn't the same person who trained the monkey," KC said. "Maybe the person who drilled the hole hid something for the other person to find. Like Dimm."

"Yeah, but when did the hole get drilled?" Marshall asked. "Was it a long time ago? Or a little while ago? It would help if we knew exactly when the stone was set into the wall."

"I know how to find out," KC said. "We can go to the Library of Congress. They keep all that Washington history there."

6
Uncovering a Secret

KC and Marshall ran to the closest Metro station and got aboard a train.

"Um, do you know where we're going?" Marshall asked.

"Sure," KC said. "The Library of Congress is near the Capitol building. We get off at the stop that says CAPITOL."

Soon they were standing in front of the massive building. A large fountain sat near the marble steps. Water poured down over a bronze man with a long beard.

"Who's that guy?" Marshall asked.

KC read a sign in front of the statue. "He's Neptune, the Roman god of the sea," she said. "Marsh, Dr. Tutu gave me an idea when he said that spider monkeys steal things. What if someone stole something valuable, then hid it in that drilled hole?"

"Then a second person—the one who trained Washington—took it out of the hole?" Marshall said.

KC nodded. "Maybe it was Dimm."

The kids ran up the steps. They found themselves in the Great Hall. It had a high, domed ceiling made of stained glass. KC peeked into her backpack. Washington was still asleep.

Light shone through the dome onto sculptures, paintings, and wall murals. A few people walked about. Their footsteps echoed in the cavernous room.

"This place is awesome!" Marshall

whispered. His voice sounded as if he were speaking in a cave.

"It's the world's largest library," KC said. "Come on, I see an information desk."

The woman behind the desk was tall with very short white hair, like a crew cut. She wore a black suit with a red rose in her lapel. A name plate on her desk said MS. MANN.

"Can I help you?" she asked KC and Marshall.

"We're studying the memorial stones in the Washington Monument," KC said. "Is there a book that tells when each stone was placed in the Monument's walls?"

"That should be easy," Ms. Mann said. "Give me a moment." She turned to a computer and typed in a few commands.

While they waited, KC read a small sign on a post near the desk. It gave the history of the building, which was built in 1897 and housed more than 17 million books.

"If you'll have a seat, Mr. Babcock will bring you a book," Ms. Mann said. She pointed to a row of desks and chairs.

"Where could we get information about unsolved crimes in Washington?" Marshall asked Ms. Mann.

"What sort of crimes?" the woman asked. "Murders? Kidnappings?"

"No, something that got stolen," said Marshall. "Like documents or money or jewels."

Ms. Mann tapped a pencil against her front teeth. "There is a Web site," she said after a moment. "Use one of our computers and type in www.stillmissing.com. The list will be long."

The kids hurried to a computer, and Marshall typed in the Web site's address. Ms. Mann was right—the list had hundreds of dates and thefts. They were all in articles taken from the *Washington Post* over the years.

KC and Marshall skipped around, reading whatever appeared on the screen. Someone stole a goat in 1901. Sheets and towels were stolen off clotheslines in 1982. One hundred bicycles were stolen in 1957.

"I'm pretty sure there wasn't a goat or a bike hidden in that memorial stone," Marshall said. He giggled.

As the kids read the list, a man came over to them. He was carrying a large

book. "Are you the one interested in the memorial stones?" he asked KC.

"Yes, thank you," KC said. "Are you Mr. Babcock?"

The man grinned. "Yes, indeed. I've been Jeremiah Babcock for seventy years." He placed the book on the desk in front of her. "I'll come fetch the book later."

Marshall pulled his chair closer to KC. The title of the book was *Carved into History: The Story of the Memorial Stones*.

KC turned to the index and found the state of Washington stone listed. When she turned to that page, she found a large picture.

"The letter *o* looks okay," Marshall said.

"I can't tell if it's been plastered over," KC said. "But look, it says the stone was set into the Monument around July 3, 1914. It's four feet long and two feet high. It weighs over eight hundred pounds."

"Okay, but that doesn't tell us who drilled a hole in it, or when," Marshall said.

"The hole was pretty small," KC said. "But maybe it went deep inside the stone. You could hide something long and thin in there." She grinned at Marshall. "Like a goat."

"More like a document or a map or a letter," Marshall said. He looked at the Web site still on the computer screen. He scrolled down till he was in the 1910s. He read silently for a minute, then he let out a loud squawk.

"Shhh, Marsh. We're gonna get thrown out of here!" KC hissed.

"Listen to this," Marshall said, reading: "Prominent jeweler Conrad Sutherland reported a robbery at his home. He told reporters that a pouch of uncut diamonds was stolen while he was out of town. Police questioned a Mr. Dusty Dimm, who was employed as a stone mason doing repairs on the Sutherland home when the diamonds went missing. Mr. Dimm was released because he was able to prove that he was away visiting his sister when the jewels were stolen. Police are still looking for the thief and the diamonds."

7

More Monkey Business

"Marsh, Dr. Tutu told us someone named Dimm brought Washington to that other vet! That means Dimm was probably the person who trained Washington to break open the memorial stone!" KC said.

"So this Dusty Dimm must have stolen the diamonds in 1914 and hidden them in the stone," Marshall said.

"And the Dimm who now owns Washington must be related to that other one," KC went on. "Dimm must have the diamonds!"

"How do we find him?" Marshall asked. "Or her."

"I don't know, but we have to get back to the White House," KC said. "Maybe the president will have an idea. Marshall, if we can track down this Dimm, we'll solve the whole mystery and find the diamonds!"

KC thanked Ms. Mann and Mr. Babcock, then she and Marshall raced out of the building. By the time the Metro train dropped them near the White House, they had calmed down.

The kids hurried through the private entrance to the White House.

They found Yvonne, the president's maid, in the kitchen reading the newspaper. "There you two are," she said. "Your folks were concerned, KC."

"Are they here?" KC asked. She leaned her backpack in a corner and unzipped the top. Washington was still asleep inside.

Yvonne shook her head. "No, but you have a very mysterious message."

Yvonne glanced at a pad next to her elbow. "A Dr. Tutu called. He said to tell you that Dr. Warren called him back after you left. Dr. Warren wanted you to have this phone number." Yvonne read off the numbers.

"But whose number is that?" KC asked.

Yvonne looked at her note. "Someone named Dimm," she said.

KC and Marshall high-fived. "We've got it!" KC cried.

"Now we can find Dimm and the diamonds!" Marshall said.

"Do you know when the president and my mom will be back?" KC asked Yvonne.

Yvonne shook her head.

KC looked at Marshall. "I can't wait," she said. "Let's call the number right now."

Yvonne got up and left the room. KC brought the phone to the table. She tapped in the numbers Yvonne had written on the pad. She listened, then asked if there was a person named Dimm there. A few seconds later, she hung up. Her face was white.

"Was it Dimm?" asked Marshall.

KC shook her head. "No, that number was for the Washington Monument."

Marshall looked stunned. "Dimm works at the Washington Monument?" he asked.

"They said they'd never heard of anyone named Dimm," KC said.

"Then why would he or she give that name to the vet?" Marshall asked.

"I don't know," KC said. "We met some park rangers over at the Washington Monument yesterday. Maybe one of them snuck the monkey in to steal the diamonds." She remembered the four rangers she and Marshall had seen while they were at the Monument.

There was Butch, Opal, Jennifer, who sold maps, and Dr. Grift. Could one of these people be the mysterious Dimm, Washington's owner and trainer?

Washington hopped out of KC's pack. He came over and crawled into her lap. KC stroked the monkey's silky fur. She thought about how the monkey had jumped on Butch, as if they were old friends. "Butch could be Washington's owner," she said to Marshall. "Washington likes him."

Marshall thought for a minute. "Yeah, and Butch seemed to know a lot about those stones. But I think the crook is Jennifer, that woman selling the maps and books. Remember she had peanuts on her counter? I found a peanut shell on the floor near that memorial stone!"

KC looked at Washington sitting on her lap. "Talk to us, Washington," she said. "Who is your owner?"

"There were two other rangers there yesterday," Marshall went on. "That woman who took us in the elevator, Opal. Washington let out a howl when he saw her with those tourists."

"Yeah, I remember now. I thought he was screeching at the tourists," KC said.

"But maybe he was screeching at her."

"Or how about Dr. Grift?" Marshall said. "He sure was in a hurry to get the monkey out of the Monument!"

Just then the president and KC's mom walked into the kitchen.

"There you are," the president said.

"KC, is that a monkey?" her mother asked, stepping back.

KC held him up. "His name is Washington," she said.

"He's lovely, honey," the president said. "But what's he doing in our kitchen?"

8

Surprise Party

"It's a long story," KC said. "You guys should sit down."

"Oh, *that* kind of story," the president said. He pulled out chairs for Lois and himself.

"Want to hold Washington, Mom?" KC asked.

"I don't think so," her mother said.

"I do," the president said.

KC handed Washington to the president. The monkey settled back on his lap and played with his red necktie.

With Marshall helping her, KC told her parents everything, starting with the white lights they'd noticed in the Washington Monument windows.

It took KC fifteen minutes to explain everything. When she was done, they all sat staring at the monkey in the president's lap.

"So you think this little chap found those diamonds and handed them over to his owner?" the president asked. "Someone named Dimm?"

KC nodded. She was tired of talking.

"And this Dimm may be related to the original Dimm, the one who probably stole the diamonds in 1914?" KC's mother asked.

KC nodded again.

"So if Dimm works in the Washington Monument, he or she could be one of the park rangers," the president added.

"We met four of them yesterday," Marshall said.

"But the thief could be someone else from a different shift," the president said. "There are about a dozen rangers working at the Monument."

"How do we find the right one?" Lois asked.

"I have an idea," KC said. "Mom, can we have a party here tomorrow?"

"What kind of party?" her mother asked.

"For all the park rangers from the Washington Monument," KC said. "We could get them all together, then I'll bring Washington in. Maybe he'll recognize Dimm!"

"Or whatever his or her real name is," the president said. "I like it. Lois, what do you say, can you get the staff to pull it off by tomorrow?"

"Yes, I think so," Lois said. "But what reason will I give for this party?"

The president scratched his chin. "I know! Tell them we all enjoy seeing the Monument from the White House windows, and we'd like to thank them for doing such a great job," he said.

"That's a good idea," KC's mom said. "And it's the truth. I love how pretty the building looks at night."

The next day, ten park rangers came to the White House. "They look different in regular clothes," Marshall said to KC.

"Let's go say hi," KC said. They ran over to greet the rangers.

Butch was wearing a bright yellow

and green tropical shirt. His aftershave smelled like lime juice.

Dr. Grift had on a suit and tie. He seemed a little nervous. His face was red and his hand, when he shook KC's, was damp.

The woman named Opal looked pretty in a pink sundress. She had pearls around her neck and her hair was tied with a scarf. A pink bag was slung over one shoulder.

Jennifer, who sold maps and books, wore a white pantsuit and white sandals. Her sunglasses were pushed back in her hair.

They were all standing around in one of the smaller dining rooms. KC's mom had brought in a lot of food and cold drinks.

"Thank you for coming on such short notice," the president said. "We just came up with this idea yesterday."

"Please help yourselves," KC's mom said. "Yvonne, our wonderful helper in the kitchen, has made strawberry short-cake for dessert!"

Everyone walked toward the food table and began filling plates.

"I still think it's Jennifer the peanut lady," Marshall whispered.

"No, it's Dr. Grift," KC said. "He's so jumpy he can hardly talk."

The park rangers began eating. The president and Lois chatted with their guests. KC and Marshall kept looking at the grandfather clock in the corner. When it chimed at one o'clock, KC winked at Marshall. Then she got up and left the room. She came back in a few minutes carrying Washington in her arms.

A few people noticed the newcomer.

"Oh, how cute!" one woman said. "What a darling little monkey!"

Then everyone else looked up.

Suddenly Washington shot out of KC's arms. He bounded to the table and began running. He knocked over two glasses of lemonade and galloped right through Butch's potato salad. He slid in some mustard but kept on moving.

With mayonnaise and mustard all over his paws, Washington jumped onto Opal's chest and screeched. He began rubbing his nose all over her face.

Opal turned as pink as her dress. Marshall ran over and scooped up Washington. He took him to his seat, but Washington kept struggling to get back to Opal.

"I am so sorry!" Lois said, standing up.

"Opal, please come with me and I'll get you some towels. And of course I'll have your dress cleaned." She took Opal's arm and led her out of the room.

The president also stood. "Please go on eating, everyone," he said to the other astonished guests. "I'll go with my wife to help Opal. We'll all be right back."

The president left the room. KC and Marshall followed with Washington.

Lois brought Opal to a powder room where she could clean off the mayonnaise and mustard. When she came out, the president and another man were waiting. KC and Marshall sat off to one side.

"Opal, this is Mr. Smiley of the FBI," the president said. "Please have a seat. We'd like you to tell us about Dimm and the diamonds."

Opal sat and placed her bag near her feet. She had brought a hand towel from the bathroom and was twisting it in her fingers. Finally she let out a big sigh. "Last year, I was working cleaning people's attics and basements," she said. "If I found anything good, I'd sell it on eBay. I made a living, sort of."

Opal paused and closed her eyes. "Anyway, six months ago, I found a box of books and papers," she went on. "There was this journal, like a diary. Some guy named Dusty Dimm had written it about a hundred years ago. I like old stuff, so I read the thing. There were drawings."

Opal stopped for a moment. She pulled a small black diary out of her bag and handed it to the president.

Desmond Smiley, the FBI director,

was taking notes as Opal told her story.

"This guy Dimm wrote how he stole some diamonds from a rich man he was working for," she went on. "His name was Sutherland. But Dimm was also working on the Washington Monument, helping build the thing. He knew that he'd be a suspect, so he decided to hide the diamonds inside the Monument, then lay low for a while."

Opal wiped her eyes with the towel.

"You're doing fine, Opal," the president said.

"Dimm made a hole in one of the big stones they were getting ready to put into the wall," Opal said. "The stone was from the state of Washington. Dimm drilled a hole right inside the letter *o*. He stuck the diamonds in the hole, then added a thin coat of plaster to cover it up. He drew a picture of the stone, right in that diary."

Opal looked at President Thornton. "I decided to get those diamonds. I knew I couldn't climb up there, so I bought Bingo, the monkey. I trained him to recognize the word *Washington,* and to hit the *o.* Every time he did it right, I gave him a reward. Monkeys learn fast."

"What happened to his arm?" the president asked.

"He fell one day and cracked a bone," Opal said. "I took him to the vet, but I gave her a fake name. I didn't want anyone to be able to connect me to the monkey. I guess I shouldn't have picked Dimm."

"How did Bingo get left behind in the Monument?" the FBI director asked.

"I was stupid," Opal said. "Bingo pulled out the diamonds—they were in a pouch—and gave them to me. I was so nervous I forgot his reward. He took off on me, so I left him there. I figured I'd get him the next day or something."

"Where are the diamonds now, Opal?" the president asked.

She shook her head. "In my freezer. I poured water over them in an ice tray and froze them," she said.

Mr. Smiley stood up. "Take me to your home, Opal," he said.

Opal stood up and handed the towel to KC's mom. "Thank you," she said. "I'm sorry I ruined your party."

Mr. Smiley led Opal from the room.

9
Washington Makes New Friends

Dr. Tutu invited Washington to live in the National Zoo. A few days later, KC and Marshall went to visit him. They stood in front of the giant cage filled with spider monkeys. There must have been fifty of them, swinging, chattering, and grooming each other's fur.

"How do we figure out which one is Washington?" Marshall asked. "They all look alike!"

"I don't know," KC said. "They seem happy, though, don't they?"

In every corner of the tall cage, spider monkeys were eating and playing and snoozing. There were vines for climbing and trees for making nests. KC noticed one monkey holding a tiny baby.

"Look," Marshall said. He pointed to a sign on the wall. WASHINGTON, ONE OF OUR SPIDER MONKEYS, HAS HAD AN EXCITING LIFE. HE STOLE SOME DIAMONDS, SLEPT IN THE WHITE HOUSE, AND HELPED CAPTURE A CRIMINAL.

Under the paragraph was another sentence: PLEASE DO NOT FEED THE MONKEYS.

Other people were watching the spider monkeys through the cage bars. One was a man sitting in front of an artist's easel. He was drawing one of the monkeys.

"I have an idea," KC told Marshall. She walked over to the artist. "Excuse me," she said. "Could you spare a sheet of paper and a pencil?"

"Sure," the man said. "Do you like to draw?"

KC looked at the man's beautiful sketch. "No, but I wish I could," she said.

KC laid the paper on the ground and wrote the word *Washington* in big letters.

"Great idea," Marshall said when he saw what she'd done.

KC and Marshall held the paper up to the bars of the cage. At first nothing happened. The monkeys continued racing and climbing and squeaking. Then one of them came toward the bars.

"Is it him?" Marshall whispered.

"I don't know," KC said.

The curious monkey sat in front of the paper and put his tiny hand through the

bars. Then he let out a loud chirp and began tapping on the letter *o*.

"Yep, it's Washington," KC said.

The monkey tilted his head to one side. He looked at KC and Marshall. Then he chirped loudly again.

Marshall grinned. "I think he just said, 'Hi, Marshall!'"

KC shook her head. "Wrong, Marsh. It's so obvious that he said hi to me, not you!"

"How do you know?" Marshall asked.

KC smiled. "Girls know these things," she said mysteriously.

KC walked over to the artist and returned his pencil. He was looking at them curiously. "What was that all about?" he asked.

KC laughed. "Don't ask. It's a long story!"

Did you know?

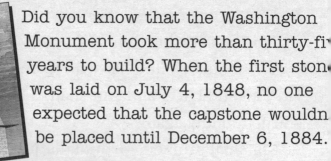

Did you know that the Washington Monument took more than thirty-fi years to build? When the first ston was laid on July 4, 1848, no one expected that the capstone wouldn be placed until December 6, 1884.

The Washington National Monument Society was low on money from the start The state of Alabama wanted to help by donating an engraved memorial stone. Th Society thought this was a great idea. The invited states and groups to donate stone to be used in building the Monument.

Many did, but it wasn't enoug Lack of funds, disagreements about the stones, and the out-break of the Civil War stoppe construction of the Monumen

During the war and for many years after the Monument stood partly finished, at a

third of its final height. Cows, pigs, and sheep wandered the grounds around it, eating grass.

The United States celebrated the one hundredth anniversary of the Declaration of Independence in July 1876. People were feeling patriotic. Congress finally came up with the money to finish the Monument. Once building started up again, it only took a few years to complete the 555-foot Monument.

Even though it was many years later, the builders included all the memorial stones that had been donated. And if you look carefully, you can still see the place where they stopped building all the way back in 1861—the marble above it is a slightly different color!

A to Z Mysteries

Help Dink, Josh, and Ruth Rose . . .

. . . **solve mysteries from A to Z**

Random House